The Story of

Little Red Riding Hood

Illustrated by Suzy-Jane Tanner

Little Red Riding Hood

Grandma

Forest

Woodcutter

It's fun to Read Along

Here's what you do-

These pictures are some of the characters and things the story tells about. Let the child to whom you are reading SEE and SAY them.

Then, as you read the story text and come to a picture instead of a word, pause and point to the picture for your listener to SEE and SAY.

You'll be amazed at how quickly children catch on and enjoy participating in the story telling.

ISBN 0-86163-791-7

Copyright © 1987 Award Publications Limited
This edition first published 1995
5th impression 2002

Published by Award Publications Limited,
27 Longford Street, London NW1 3DZ

Printed in Malaysia

Wolf

Mother

Grandma's house

Cloak

Bread and jam

Basket

There was once a little girl who was so good that her decided to make her a little red . She looked so pretty in it that everyone called her Little Red Riding Hood.

Everybody loved , especially her who lived in a little cottage on the other side of the .

One day her baked some fresh and made some . "Take these to your ," she told , "for she has been ill."

At once set out through the to , carrying the and in her . She had not gone very far down the path when she met a great big .

Now the would have liked to gobble  up there and then, but he knew that a was working nearby. "Where are you going ?" asked the . did not know how dangerous it is to speak to wolves. "I am taking some  and to , for she is ill in ," she replied.

"I shall visit poor too," said the . "We will each take a different path and see who gets there first."

The set off as fast as he could run to . stopped to pick a pretty bunch of for so, of course, the arrived first. He knocked on the .

"Who is there?" asked .

"It is I, ," answered the  in a very squeaky voice. "Come in my dear," said . "The is not locked."

When saw the  she screamed and jumped out of the . Then she ran to fetch the as fast as her  could carry her.

The put on a 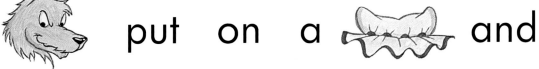 and of Grandma's to disguise

himself. Then he got into , pulled up the  and waited for to arrive.

It was not long before knocked on the .

"Who is there?" called the  in his softest voice.

"It is I, ," she replied.

"Come in my dear," said the . "The is not locked."

Poor was frightened to see her lying in looking so very different.

"Come and kiss your ," said the .

took a step closer to the . "What big you have !" she said.

"That is all the better to hear you with, my dear," replied the .

took another step

towards the  and said,

"What big 👀 you have !"

"All the better to see you

with my dear," said the 🐺.

"Come closer so that 👵 can

see how pretty you look."

 took two more steps

towards the 🛏. She was

very puzzled at the great

change in her 👵.

"What a big you have !" exclaimed .

"All the better to smell with, my dear," said the .

"Come over here and show what goodies you have in your little ."

took her with the  and that her had made. She put it on the  next to the .

"What big you have !" said .

"That, my dear, is all the better to eat you with!" cried the and with that, he jumped out of  and sprang towards  !

Just at that moment, the  flew open and in rushed the ! He had been warned about the by .

The ran out of but the brave was close behind. He chased the through the and soon killed him.

hurried back home after the . She was so pleased to hear that the wicked was dead and to find her dear waiting for her, safe and sound.